A Kitten
Called
Moonlight

For Charlotte
M. W.

For Elizabeth
C. B.

Text copyright © 2001 by Martin Waddell
Illustrations copyright © 2001 by Christian Birmingham

First U.S. edition 2001

Library of Congress Cataloging-in-Publication Data

Waddell, Martin.
A kitten called Moonlight / written by Martin Waddell ;
illustrated by Christian Birmingham — 1st U.S. ed.
p. cm.
Summary: A little girl and her mother recall how a special
kitten came into their lives one dark and stormy night.
ISBN 0-7636-1176-X
[1. Cats — Fiction. 2. Mother and child — Fiction.]
I. Birmingham, Christian, ill.   II. Title.
PZ7.W1137 K1   2001   [e] — dc21   99-088329

10 9 8 7 6 5 4 3 2 1

Printed in Italy

This book was typeset in Calligraphic.
The illustrations were done in chalk pastel.

Candlewick Press
2067 Massachusetts Avenue
Cambridge, Massachusetts 02140

MARTIN WADDELL

A Kitten Called Moonlight

Illustrated by

CHRISTIAN BIRMINGHAM

CANDLEWICK PRESS
CAMBRIDGE, MASSACHUSETTS

"I'd like my story again," Charlotte said.
"Which story?" asked Mommy.
"The one I like best, about Moonlight
    and me," Charlotte said.
"I thought that's the one it might be,"
    Mommy said.

"Once there was a white kitten called Moonlight," Mommy said.

"We don't know he was called Moonlight," Charlotte said.
"We just know he got lost."

"That's right," Mommy said, "the little kitten was lost and alone, and wandering around. It was a cold winter night."

"The little kitten was crying," said Charlotte. "Maybe he wanted someone to find him."

"Maybe he did. We don't know.
  Then a big something came."

"It was a car," Charlotte said.

"I'll bet the little kitten had never
  seen a car before," Mommy said.
"He was scared and he hid. The car
  lights shone into the dark. And
  there were two shiny bright eyes.
  Somebody saw them."

"I know who saw them!"
  said Charlotte.

"It was a little girl," Mommy said. "She had been to a party. The little girl told her mommy she had seen something move in the dark."

"'There's something down there by the boats,'" Charlotte said. "That's what the little girl told her mommy."

"Yes," Mommy said. "But her mommy hurried her into the house. She didn't want her to catch cold."

"What happened then?" asked Charlotte.

"The little girl had her supper and her mommy put her to bed. Later she came to see if the little girl was asleep."

"But the little girl's bed was empty," said Charlotte. "The quilt was thrown right back, and the little girl wasn't there. 'My goodness, where can she be?' thought her mommy."

"Something like that," Mommy said. "Her mommy searched all over the house."

"I like this part," Charlotte said.

"She found the little girl curled up by the window, gazing out at the dark sea and the moonlight that shone on the shore. 'What are you doing up out of bed?' asked her mommy."

"'There's something down there by the sea. I *know* that there is.' That's what the little girl told her mommy," said Charlotte.

"Yes, she did," Mommy said, "and her mommy didn't believe there was. But she thought for a minute and said, 'We'll take a look to make sure.'"

"The little girl and her mommy went down to the shore," Charlotte said.

"Yes," Mommy said. "They searched and they searched but they couldn't find anything. 'Something *was* here,' said the little girl."

"She knew she was right," Charlotte said.

"Yes," Mommy said. "But her mommy still didn't believe her. She told the little girl, 'We'll take one more look, just in case.'"

"The little girl and her mommy walked out on the rocks. There was only the moonlight to see by. They walked right out by the edge of the sea — and what do you think they saw there?"

"It was a kitten!" said Charlotte.

"A little white kitten," said Mommy, "all thin and bony and cold. It was on a rock with the sea splashing around it. The poor little kitten was hungry and scared. The little girl and her mommy got splashed. But they rescued the kitten . . .

and the little girl carried him
all the way home."

"She gave the kitten some warm milk and he went to sleep in her arms. And after a while the little girl felt sleepy too, and her mommy carried her and the kitten upstairs. She tucked the little girl in her bed, all cozy and—"

"You've forgotten the best part,"
said Charlotte. "Her mommy said
if no one owned the kitten they
could keep him forever. She said
they should find a good name for
the kitten and the little girl knew
right away what it should be.
'Moonlight would be a good name,'
she told her mommy. 'We'd never
have found him without the
moonlight.'"

"So that's what they called their
kitten," Mommy said. "Now you've
told me the end of your story."

"We love that story, don't we, Moonlight?"
Charlotte said.
"And I know why," said Mommy.
"We love it because it's about us,"
Charlotte said. "Moonlight
and Mommy and me."